CONTENTS

Chapter 1
Foot

Chick and Brain

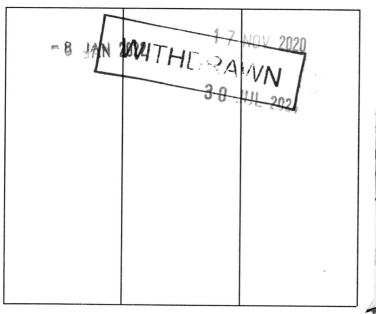

WALKER
BOOKS

No, Brain, no.
I say *Hello, Brain.*
Then *you* say
Hello, Chick.

Like this:

Hello, Chick.

3

4

But I will not smell your foot until you say **PLEASE**.

Like this: *Please* smell my foot.

Oh! OK!

9

That is much better!

Now I will smell your foot.

SNIFF!

Chapter 2
Spot

19

You did not say *hello.*

You did not say *please*!

Like this: *Hello,* Spot. *Please* smell my foot.

Thank you, Spot.

Mmmm . . .

Um . . . Spot? SPOT!

You have to say *you're welcome*!

Oh! You're yummy! I mean *you're welcome*!

It does smell good.

But it does *not* smell great.

Yeah. I know.

Wait. *What?*

Chapter 3
Lunch

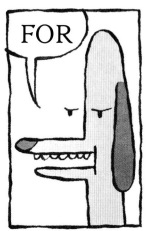
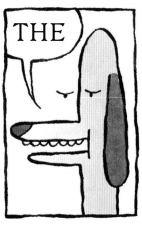

Here you go!

Mmmm . . .

🎵 Don't forget to say *thank you for the pepper!* 🎵

39

40

41

What *now*?

Someone is at your door.

Please go and see.

Grrrr. I will go and see.

Oh, *Spot.* You did not say *excuse me.*

You must say *excuse me* before you leave the table.

Don't do it, Spot! Brain did not say *please*!

Good grief, Chick! I am trying to help you!

That is nice. But you must say *please*.

48

Chapter 4
Other Foot

55

You see, my other foot does not smell good.

My other foot does not smell great.

My other foot smells bad. Really, *really* bad.

Really?

You did?

Yeah. I *know* I did.

Look. Spot said that your foot smelled like chicken.

Yes. That was nice. Spot made me feel good.

Then he invited
you to lunch.

Yes. That was
nice, too. Spot
made me feel
special.

No! No, no, NO!

I know that Spot is a DOG!

Yes. I know that, too.

Do you know what dogs eat?

Dog food?

You *are* very smart!

Yeah.
I know.

Look, Jerry Kalback, look!
This book is for you.

First published in Great Britain 2020 by Walker Books Ltd
87 Vauxhall Walk, London SE11 5HJ

2 4 6 8 10 9 7 5 3 1

This book was typeset in JHA My Happy 70s

Printed and bound in China

British Library Cataloguing in Publication Data:
a catalogue record for this book is
available from the British Library

ISBN 978-1-4063-9246-3

www.walker.co.uk